**A Marc Brown ARTHUR Chapter Book**

# Arthur and the
# Cootie-Catcher

Text by Stephen Krensky

Based on a teleplay by Joe Fallon

Little, Brown and Company

Boston   New York   London

For our terrific editor,
Laura Marsh

First Edition

The characters and events portrayed in this book are fictitious. Any
similarity to real persons, living or dead, is coincidental and not intended
by the author.

Arthur® is a registered trademark of Marc Brown.

Text has been reviewed and assigned a reading level by Laurel S. Ernst,
M.A., Teachers College, Columbia University, New York, New York;
reading specialist, Chappaqua, New York

Library of Congress Cataloging-in-Publication Data

Brown, Marc.
    Arthur and the cootie-catcher / text by Stephen Krensky ; based on
a teleplay by Jon Fallon.—1st ed.
      p.   cm.—(A Marc Brown Arthur chapter book)
    Summary: At Prunella's half-birthday party, her sister unveils a
fortune-telling cootie-catcher that seems to be able to predict the future.
      ISBN 0-316-11993-8 (hc).—ISBN 0-316-12266-1 (pb)
    [1. Fortune telling—Fiction.  2. Aardvark—Fiction.]  I. Arthur
(Television program)  II. Title.  III. Series: Brown, Marc Tolon.
Marc Brown Arthur chapter book.
PZ7.K883Aq   1999
[Fic]—dc21                                                          98-52061

10 9 8 7 6 5 4 3

WOR (hc)
COM-MO (pb)

Printed in the United States of America

# Chapter 1

• • • • • • • • • • •

"I see the party's started already," said Francine.

She and Arthur had just arrived at Prunella's house, and judging by the noise, they were the last to get there.

The backyard was decorated for a birthday party — with balloons and streamers — or at least half of it was. The other half was bare, as though someone had drawn a line down the middle of the yard and only paid attention to one side.

Arthur nodded. "I'm still a little confused about this," he said. "It hasn't been a year since Prunella had her last birthday party."

"I know," said Francine. "It's been six months. That's why this is her *half-*birthday party." She pointed to the half-decorated table where half of a large cake sat in the middle.

"Oh, I see," said Arthur, who wasn't sure he really did.

They joined the rest of their friends, including Binky, Buster, Muffy, Sue Ellen, and the Brain. They had gathered around Prunella to give her their presents.

"I'm so glad all of you could come," she said. "As you can see," she added, waving at the decorations, "this is my half-birthday."

"I hope the cake isn't half-baked," Buster said to Binky.

Prunella just smiled at him. "Under the circumstances, my sister thought maybe I should only invite half of you, but I decided to invite all of you for half as long instead."

"All this half stuff is giving me a headache," Arthur whispered to Francine.

"You'll feel better if you only half listen," Francine whispered back. "That's what's working for me."

"Prunella," said Binky, "since this is your half-birthday, I got you this . . ."

He handed her half of a baseball.

Prunella laughed. "Perfect for all my half-hearted attempts to play."

Buster was next. He gave her an opened chocolate bar. Half of it had been eaten already.

"Gee," said Prunella. "Tooth marks and everything."

Buster swallowed what he was chewing before he spoke. "I did my best to get this just right," he said.

"Thanks," said Prunella, holding the candy bar at arm's length. "I'll save this for when I'm really hungry."

Sue Ellen was next.

"I thought about giving you half a bracelet," she said. "But then I realized it would keep falling off your arm. So, instead, I got you this."

She held out an autographed poster of a football player.

The Brain scratched his head. "But you're giving her the *whole* picture."

"Don't worry," said Sue Ellen. "It's okay — he's a *halfback*."

Arthur groaned.

"All right everyone!" called out Prunella's big sister, Rubella, from behind them. "Step aside. Stand back. Give me some room."

She had come out the back door holding a tray in front of her. There was something on the tray, but it was covered by a cloth.

The birthday guests parted to let her through.

"Gather round!" said Rubella. "But not too close."

Everyone inched forward.

"Pay careful attention," she went on in a deep voice. "The moment has come."

"What moment?" asked Buster.

Rubella smiled mysteriously. "The moment," she said, "that will change your lives forever."

# Chapter 2

• • • • • • • • • • • •

As Rubella looked around, everyone looked at her intently.

"I don't think I've ever had my life changed forever before," said Buster. "I wonder what it feels like."

"You'll find out soon enough," said Rubella. She removed the cloth from the tray, revealing a many-sided paper object.

"Paper?" said Francine. "Paper is going to change my life? I don't think so."

"Not just paper," Rubella explained. "This is a fortune-teller's cootie-catcher."

The kids laughed.

Rubella waved one long finger at them.

"Make fun at your own risk. This was created with a rare, mystical folding process. You don't want to anger it."

She opened and closed the cootie-catcher several times. The kids all moved forward for a better look.

"The technique was passed down from our ancestors, Transylvanian commuters of the Carpathian Mountains."

"Wow!" said Buster. "I wonder if they had traffic jams back then."

Rubella ignored him. "It has the power," she went on, "to tell fortunes when given to a special girl upon her half-birthday."

Bowing to Prunella, Rubella carefully placed the cootie-catcher on her sister's fingers. Prunella's eyes widened as she stared at it.

"Okay, okay," said Francine. "If we're done here, can I have some cake?"

"Scoff if you will," said Rubella. "But dare you ask it to foretell your future?"

Francine shrugged. "Sure. Can it tell me if I'll play professional football?"

"First, you have to pick a color," said Prunella.

"Green," said Francine.

"G-R-E-E-N," said Prunella, as she opened and closed the cootie-catcher five times.

"Now pick a number," said Rubella.

Francine looked at the numbers on the inside of the cootie-catcher. "Three," she said.

"One-two-three," said Prunella, moving the cootie-catcher three times. "And finally, pick one last number."

"Six," said Francine.

Prunella lifted the flap marked "6." "It says, '*Yes.*' That means you will play professional football."

"Amazing!" said Buster. "You'll be famous."

Francine frowned. "Maybe. But I'll have to wait till I grow up to find out for sure."

"The cootie-catcher doesn't share our concerns with time and space," said Rubella. "It just answers the questions."

"Maybe a question about today or tomorrow . . ." said Muffy.

"I've got one!" shouted Buster.

"Go ahead," said Rubella.

"Will I get an 'A' on the next geography test?"

"You never get 'A's' in geography, Buster," Arthur reminded him. "You have a terrible sense of direction."

"Yeah," said the Brain. "You can get lost on the way to the bathroom."

Rubella held up her hand. "It's still a fair question," she said. "Pick a color, Buster, and then two numbers."

"Blue," said Buster, watching Prunella closely. "Then two . . . and five."

Prunella opened the "5" flap. *"It is certain,"* she informed him.

Everyone laughed, including Buster.

"Oh, come on," he said. "I don't even get 'A's' in my alphabet soup."

"We need another question," said Francine. "A tough one."

"I know!" said Arthur. "Will Binky sing a stupid song in front of everyone tomorrow?"

Binky frowned. "What kind of question is that?"

"Tough," said Francine. "Very tough. We've heard you sing."

Prunella worked the cootie-catcher as Arthur made his choices.

"So what's the answer?" asked Muffy.

Prunella lifted the flap. *"Yes, definitely,"* she said.

Francine and Arthur looked shocked.

"No way!" they said together.

Rubella folded her arms. "You'll see," she said. "The cootie-catcher has spoken."

# Chapter 3

• • • • • • • • • • • •

The next day at school, Mr. Ratburn handed back the geography tests to the class.

"A lot of you seemed to have taken this test in your sleep," he said.

"Uh, oh," said Arthur.

Mr. Ratburn continued to walk around, returning the tests.

"As for you, Buster . . ." he declared.

Buster shrank into his seat.

"Unusually good work. Congratulations!"

Buster's test had a big red "A" at the top.

Arthur's mouth dropped open. So did Francine's. And Binky's.

"Wow!" Buster whispered. "The cootie-catcher was right."

Arthur, Binky, Francine, Muffy, the Brain, and Buster were still talking about the cootie-catcher that afternoon in gym class.

"It still seems impossible," said Francine.

"I agree it's not *likely*," said the Brain. "But *impossible*—obviously not."

Arthur looked across the gym.

"Uh, oh," he said. "The coaches are at it again. They're always arguing about something."

Coach Bumpus and Coach Grimslid were waving their arms in disagreement.

"The last line is *up the spout again*," said Coach Grimslid.

"No, it's *down the spout again*," insisted Coach Bumpus. He waved his arm at Binky. "Barnes, come here!"

Binky ran right over. There was nothing he wouldn't do for his coaches.

"Barnes, we're having a small difference of opinion here. Maybe you can help us out."

"Okay." Binky was ready. "What do you need? Push-ups? Sit-ups?"

Coach Grimslid folded her arms. "That's the Lakewood spirit, Barnes. But we need something a little different. Do you know the 'Eensy Weensy Spider' song?"

Binky stopped to think. "The one about the eensy weensy spider?"

"Yes, that's it," said Coach Bumpus. "Now, do you remember the words?"

Binky nodded.

"Excellent. Could you sing them for us?"

"Here?" said Binky. "Now?"

"We're counting on you, Barnes. Don't let us down."

15

Binky puffed out his chest. "Yes, sir!" He took a deep breath and began to sing.

> *The eensy weensy spider*
> *went up the water spout.*
> *Down came the rain*
> *and washed the spider out.*

As Binky's voice rang out, Arthur and the others suddenly stopped talking. They stared at him across the gym floor.

> *Out came the sun*
> *and dried up all the rain*
> *so the eensy weensy spider*
> *went up the spout again.*

"Aha!" shouted Coach Grimslid. "You see? I told you."

"Okay, okay," said Coach Bumpus. "So you were right this time. Don't let it go to your head."

"Do you want me to sing anything else?" asked Binky.

"No, no," said Coach Grimslid. "You did a fine job, but one song is quite enough, thank you. You can fall in with the others."

Binky walked back across the gym, beaming.

"Why are you all staring at me like that?" he asked the others.

"Because you sang a silly song," said Arthur.

"Just like the cootie-catcher predicted," said Francine.

Binky stopped in his tracks. It was true. He had done exactly that.

"Now what happens?" he asked.

"I don't know," said Francine. "But we all know who *does*."

# Chapter 4

In Prunella's backyard that afternoon, kids were lined up to ask the cootie-catcher for opinions on everything.

"Each of you may ask only one question a day," said Rubella, monitoring the crowd. "The process is too draining to do any more."

Prunella nodded, pressing the back of her hand against her forehead.

"I grow weary," she sighed.

"Will I own a dog?" asked Buster." No, I mean a snake. No, a snake farm . . ."

"Should I loan Buster some money?" asked Francine.

"Will I live in Tibet?" asked Sue Ellen.

"Will I go to college in Paris?" asked Muffy.

"Will I ever command my own fleet of submarines?" asked Arthur.

Prunella's fingers got a workout as the cootie-catcher did its stuff. The corners opened and shut in a constant blur.

"That's all for now!" she announced finally. "The cootie-catcher and I need a rest."

The crowd broke up and headed for the Sugar Bowl. Just outside the shop, Francine turned to Buster.

"Why did you ask me for money?" she said. "You don't need it."

"But I do," Buster insisted. He turned his empty pockets inside out. "I can't get a soda unless you loan me something."

Francine was not convinced. "I asked the cootie-catcher if you needed money, using up my question for today. And it said '*No.*' "

She turned up her nose and walked inside.

Buster turned to leave just as a woman overloaded with packages came up to him.

"Excuse me, young man . . ." she began.

A few minutes later, Buster rushed inside the Sugar Bowl. He was waving a dollar.

"A lady gave me this to help her carry some bags."

"You see?" said Francine. "The cootie-catcher was right again. You didn't need my money, after all."

Everyone but the Brain nodded solemnly at this latest proof of the cootie-catcher's power. He, however, just sat back, shaking his head.

Later, when everyone was leaving, the Brain walked out with Arthur.

"Arthur?" he said.

"What?"

"I hope you don't believe all this mumbo jumbo. Everything that's happened is just a coincidence." He paused. "Or perhaps a series of coincidences."

"What do you mean?"

The Brain sighed. "A cootie-catcher, a simple contraption of folded paper, cannot predict the future."

Arthur gasped. "Don't say that!"

"Why not?"

Arthur looked around. "Quiet," he whispered. "Rubella says that anyone who doesn't listen to the cootie-catcher will be cursed."

The Brain shook his head. "Come on, Arthur, you don't really believe that. We left all that stuff behind in the Dark Ages. Now, in the bright light of science, we march forward, examining and exploring the new frontiers of—"

*Cccruuunnnccchhhh!*

At that moment a big truck backed up, crushing a bike against a tree.

"My bike!" said the Brain.

Arthur gasped. "It's the curse of the cootie-catcher!" he said. "Right on schedule."

# Chapter 5

· · · · · · · · · · ·

At school, Prunella walked down the hall gazing into space. Sue Ellen and Francine came running up behind her.

Sue Ellen tapped her on the shoulder.

"Don't bother me," said Prunella. "You don't have an appointment."

"Sorry," said Sue Ellen. "I was just wondering when I can get my fortune told again."

Prunella sighed. "When the birds begin their song and the new sun casts long shadows."

She walked away dreamily.

Sue Ellen frowned for a moment. "Oh,"

she said finally, "you mean tomorrow morning?"

"What about me?" asked Francine. "I didn't play football yesterday afternoon even though everyone begged me to. Should I do that again?"

Prunella shrugged. "Who can say?"

"I was hoping you could," said Francine. "That's why I'm asking."

"Oh, Francine, Francine. . . . It touches me to think you are trying to wrestle with the mysteries of the universe."

"I'm really not wrestling," said Francine. "I just want answers."

"Well, I don't have them now. Even when you hold the key that unlocks the secrets of the future, sometimes the key needs polishing."

Francine frowned. "What does that mean?"

"It means I'm tired," said Prunella. "Check back with me later."

But Prunella found little time for rest, even on her way home from school. As she walked down the street, a crowd of kids followed behind her.

"Should I buy a new bike?" the Brain asked meekly.

"We'll see," said Prunella.

As she passed Arthur's house, D.W. was hanging over the fence.

"Can I get my fortune told?" she called out.

Prunella shook her head. "Sorry. A child's worry is a drop of rain in a sea of tears."

D.W. made a face. "That's the dumbest thing I've ever heard."

"Ssssh!" said Arthur. "You don't want to get cursed."

"I don't care about any old curse," said D.W. "Besides, I don't know what a curse is."

"I'll explain it to you," the Brain said sadly.

As he took D.W. aside, Muffy rode up on her bike.

"Hey," she said, "who wants to come over to my house and play computer games?"

"Sorry."

"Not today."

"Maybe another time."

Muffy looked surprised. Nobody ever turned down the chance to play at her house. "You know," she went on, "the games you love. All the latest technology. I've got a new joystick. Hello?"

Everyone ignored her. All eyes remained on Prunella.

"Who can think of mere toys," she said, "when so many fates hang in the balance."

"Well, sure," said Muffy, "fates are important. But we've got snacks, too.

Arthur? Buster? Anyone? We just got a big delivery from the supermarket. You can have make-your-own sundaes. And if you're not interested in games, we can watch movies on my big-screen TV."

Prunella turned to the right, and all the kids followed her. Muffy stopped pedaling and watched them disappear around the corner.

She sighed. "They don't know what they're missing," she said, and pedaled away in the opposite direction.

# Chapter 6

• • • • • • • • • • • •

"It was my pitch. I could have hit it," said the Brain.

"I know," said Arthur. "I know."

Buster sighed. "But what could you do? The cootie-catcher had spoken. It told you not to swing at any pitches."

The three of them were standing on the playground. Arthur and Buster were trying to cheer up the Brain, who had struck out three times during that day's baseball game.

"It was bad enough to strike out," said the Brain. "But not being allowed to swing . . . !"

"Hey," said Buster. "The cootie-catcher has its reasons. All we can do is follow its advice."

"Not true," said Muffy, riding up behind them. "Now you have a choice."

"What do you mean?" asked Arthur.

"I'll show you," said Muffy, removing a glittery bundle from her bike basket.

"What's that?" asked the Brain.

Muffy smiled. "Just a little something I had made for me. It's a deluxe, Crosswire Platinum Series Cootie-Catcher."

"Is that good?" asked Buster.

"Better than good," Muffy assured him. "It has all-new, better fortunes designed by me personally."

Her friends looked doubtful.

"But it's not your half-birthday," the Brain reminded her.

"And did you use the rare, mystical folding process?" asked Buster.

Muffy waved away their concerns.

"This," she insisted, "is the best cootie-catcher money can buy. Come on, ask it anything."

"All right," said Buster. He thought for a moment. "Should I study for the next test?"

Muffy moved the cootie-catcher back and forth. Glitter and powder shot out. Arthur sneezed.

Buster stepped back in alarm. "So what does it say?"

Muffy looked down. *"You will be very rich,"* she said.

"That's nice, I guess," said Buster. "But what about the test?"

"Hey, what could be better than knowing you'll be rich?" said Muffy. She turned to Arthur. "What about you, Arthur? Come on, ask it!"

"Okay, okay," said Arthur. "Um, I've been wanting some new sneakers. Will I get them soon?"

Muffy put the cootie-catcher through its paces.

"It says: *Spend today like there's no tomorrow.*"

Arthur frowned. "I wasn't thinking about spending. I was hoping to get the sneakers as a gift."

Muffy rolled her eyes. "Picky, picky, picky. Hey, if you follow this advice, you'll be *swimming* in sneakers." She turned to the Brain. "All right, it's your turn."

"Very well," said the Brain. "Will the stock market go up this year?"

Muffy moved the cootie-catcher back and forth.

"It says: *Money doesn't grow on trees.*" She beamed at them. "Isn't this great? We could keep doing this all day."

"Not likely," said the Brain.

"Definitely not," said Arthur.

"In your dreams," said Buster.

"I don't get it," said Muffy. "This cootie-catcher is fancier than Prunella's, and it will make you rich. What more do you three want, anyway?"

"The right answers!" her friends said together. Then they walked away.

# Chapter 7

• • • • • • • • • • • • •

The kids were all lined up at Prunella's again. They wanted to ask more questions. A few had brought toys or books that had something to do with what they wanted to know. But only Binky was holding a teddy bear.

"Gee, Binky," said the Brain. "That's an interesting look for you."

Binky's face turned red. "The cootie-catcher told me to carry my good luck charm everywhere. What was I supposed to do? Risk the curse?"

"No, no," said the Brain. "You did the

right thing. Of course," he added, covering his mouth, "it does look a little funny."

Binky made a face. "Tell me about it. Do you know what it feels like to carry around a teddy bear everywhere you go? One kid asked me if I had seen Goldilocks. Another wanted to know if we were going to hibernate this winter."

"Is the bear at least bringing you good luck?" asked Buster.

Binky shook his head. "Only if you think it's good luck to have traffic stop for you because drivers are so busy pointing and laughing."

The Brain nodded. "So why have you brought it back?"

"I'm hoping the cootie-catcher will change its mind."

"Good luck," said the Brain.

"What about me?" asked Francine. "I won a free ice-cream cone today and I couldn't take it. Why? Because the cootie-catcher said I should be paying for everything."

"QUIET DOWN!" Rubella shouted out the back door. "Show some respect at the shrine of the cootie-catcher."

"The shrine?" asked Binky. "Is there one of those giant gongs?"

"Ssssh!" said Arthur. "Remember the curse."

"You need to speak softly," Rubella went on. "Prunella is exhausted."

"Keeping all these cosmic connections must be hard," said the Brain.

"She probably has to eat a lot to keep her strength up," said Buster.

At that moment Prunella staggered to the door.

"Rubella's right!" Buster whispered to Arthur. "She does look tired."

"And pale," Arthur added.

"It's gone!" Prunella wailed.

Nobody had to ask what she was referring to. It had to be the cootie-catcher.

Binky looked at his teddy bear and gasped. "Now I'll never be free," he whispered.

"It can't be gone," said Francine. "When's the last time you remember seeing it?"

Prunella closed her eyes, trying to remember. "I had it in my room this morning."

"That's not much help," said Muffy. "Your room always looks like a bomb just went off in it."

Prunella ignored her.

"Did I take it to school? I'm pretty sure I did."

"Call the police!" said the Brain. "Call the FBI, the FDA, and the BBC."

"That will take too long," said Arthur. "Let's form a search party."

"We need to retrace Prunella's steps today!" said Francine. "Wherever she's been, we have to go."

Prunella slumped down on the ground. "Hurry," she whispered. "My powers are failing."

# Chapter 8

• • • • • • • • • • • •

The kids quickly spread out all over town. They retraced Prunella's route to school, but found nothing. When they reached the school itself, they went to see Mr. Haney in his office.

"I didn't expect to see any of you here at this time of day," he said. "It's almost five o'clock."

"We think we left something here," said Francine. "We just want to check."

Mr. Haney nodded. "Well, don't take too long. We'll be closing up for the day in a little while."

The kids looked in the classroom, around Prunella's locker, the gym, and the cafeteria. They found three pieces of old homework, two wads of chewed gum, and half a yo-yo.

"I've been looking for that yo-yo," said Binky. He gave his teddy bear a little hug. "Maybe you are good luck after all."

"Now what?" asked Francine.

"We go back and hope somebody else found it."

"Do you think the cootie-catcher could curse us for not finding it?" asked Buster.

"N-no," said Arthur, but his voice was a little shaky.

Prunella and Rubella were still in the yard when the others returned.

"Any luck?" asked Prunella. "No, don't bother telling me. I can tell by your faces."

"It wasn't there," said Francine.

"But all is not lost," said Muffy. "You

can use mine, Prunella." She pulled out her cootie-catcher, spreading glitter and powder on everyone.

The kids groaned.

"Only the one she got on her half-birthday has the power," said Rubella.

"Then we're doomed," said Arthur. "We're like . . ."

"A car without a steering wheel," said Francine.

"A ship without a rudder," said the Brain.

"A TV with no remote," said Buster.

Suddenly, Prunella's mother called to her from the porch.

"Did you want this, Pruney? I found it mixed in with some clothes in the wash."

She held up a dripping wad of paper.

Prunella ran to her.

"It's the cootie-catcher!" she cried.

The Brain took a closer look. "Or it was," he said.

Francine put her ear up to the cootie-catcher. "Maybe we can still save it. Maybe it's not too late. I need tweezers, scissors, tape, and, most important—"

"Yes?" said Prunella.

"A blow dryer."

The tools were quickly assembled. Then Francine went to work. Nobody dared to speak as the operation progressed.

"Tweezers."

"Scissors."

"Tape."

At crucial moments, the blow dryer was turned on and off. "Thank goodness there's a 'fluff' setting," said Francine.

Finally, she was done.

"Give it a try," said Francine. "But gently. It's been through a lot."

Prunella carefully put the cootie-catcher on her fingers.

"You'll have to expect a little stiffness at

first," Francine cautioned her. "But that will go away over time."

Prunella looked down. She flexed her fingers and the cootie-catcher opened and shut.

"It still works!" she said.

Everyone cheered.

"To celebrate," said Arthur, "let's all go to my house and watch TV. *Turtles! Turtles! Turtles!* is coming on."

# Chapter 9

• • • • • • • • • • • •

As the kids approached Arthur's house, Buster described last week's episode.

"The turtles were swimming in a lake," Buster explained. "And there was this underwater shot of a sunken boat or something. Then—"

"Wait a minute!" said the Brain suddenly. "Before we watch, shouldn't we find out if that's the right thing to do?"

"Why wouldn't it be?" asked Muffy. "We watch that show every week."

"But we didn't used to have anything to check with," said Prunella. "Now we do." She paused. "Let me gather my strength."

"That's right," said Francine. "And after the close call we just had, we wouldn't want to make any mistakes."

"Do your stuff, Prunella," said Buster.

A short while later, the kids were sitting on the curb. They weren't talking or laughing or even looking at one another. They were just sitting.

D.W. saw them when she looked out the window.

"Arthur, what are you doing out there?" she shouted. "Come on in. *Turtles! Turtles! Turtles!* is starting."

Arthur sighed. "We know!" he shouted back. "But the cootie-catcher says we shouldn't watch it."

"But it's never even seen the show," D.W. reminded them.

"That doesn't matter," said Francine. "The cootie-catcher is all-knowing."

D.W. laughed. "Well, I'm glad I wasn't there when you asked."

The Brain put up his hands to cover the cootie-catcher.

"Don't let it hear you say that, D.W.!" he cautioned her. "You might be cursed."

D.W. shook her head. "That thing doesn't look like it could hurt a fly. Oops, sorry. Can't talk now — the show is starting."

From the curb, everyone could hear the TV faintly. Buster turned to look at the window.

"Maybe I can see something in the reflection," he muttered.

"Careful!" Francine told him. "You don't want to be cursed."

Nobody wanted to be cursed. So they just continued to sit there, fidgeting.

Finally, Arthur jumped up.

"I can't take this anymore. I feel silly. Why are we doing this?"

Everyone looked at him in shock.

"Should we be blindly obeying some old, folded piece of paper?" he went on. "Or should we be making our own decisions?"

"No, no. Blind is good," said Buster.

"Very good," the Brain added.

"I realize that we may make mistakes," said Arthur. "But we were doing okay before."

"Could you step back a little, Arthur?" asked Buster. "I don't want any of your curse sloshing over onto me."

"Hold on," said Francine.

"You don't agree with Arthur, do you?" asked Prunella.

Francine laughed. "Of course not. But he has given me an idea. Why don't we ask the cootie-catcher whether we should listen to it anymore?"

"Yeah!" said Muffy. "Let's see what it says."

"You're missing the point," Arthur insisted.

"Quiet, Arthur," said the Brain. "And just be glad you haven't been hit by a truck yet like my bike."

"Buster," said Francine, "you pick a color and then the numbers."

Buster looked around, thinking. He noticed Arthur's yellow sweater.

"Yellow," he said.

Everyone watched Prunella's fingers. When it was time to pick a number, Buster spoke again.

"Two," he said.

Prunella opened and shut the cootie-catcher twice.

"Should we stop listening to you?" asked Francine.

"Look under 2," said Buster.

They all leaned forward as Prunella lifted the flap.

"*Yes, definitely,*" it said.

The Brain started dancing around. "Free at last!" he cried. "Free at last!"

# Chapter 10

• • • • • • • • • • • •

"Come on," said Buster. "Let's go watch *Turtles! Turtles! Turtles!* before they go back in their shells."

The kids all rushed to the door. They could hear the voice coming from the TV.

*"Turtles are the oldest living reptile group. Some are over seven feet long. Baby turtles' shells are not yet hardened like the armored shells of their mother. Look out, little turtles!"*

"Hurry," said Buster. "We don't want to miss the best part."

They all shuffled in. As Prunella passed the wastebasket, she dropped the cootie-catcher in it.

"It was fun while it lasted," she said. "But wrestling with the mysteries of the universe can be very tiring."

Later that night, Mrs. Read looked up the stairs. D.W.'s light was still on.

"D.W., what are you doing still up? Turn off your light and go to sleep."

"In a minute," said D.W.

Inside her room, D.W. was sitting cross-legged on her bed. In her hand was Prunella's crumpled cootie-catcher.

"Can I go to sleep now?" she asked, opening the flap.

"*No,*" it said.

"How about in an hour?" D.W. asked.

She moved the cootie-catcher back and forth.

"*Definitely not.*"

D.W. sighed. "What about two hours?" she whispered. "Three? Come on, give me a break."

Outside, the moon was rising and the night was still, except for the sound coming from D.W.'s open window, of a cootie-catcher opening and closing over and over again.

# How to Make a Cootie-Catcher

1. Fold a square piece of paper (for example, trim an 8½" x 11" sheet to 8½" x 8½") in half diagonally and open.

2. Fold the other diagonal and open.

3. Fold each corner in toward the center, and crease.

4. Flip the paper over.

5. Fold each corner toward the center.

6. Fold in half vertically and open.

7. Fold in half horizontally.

8. Using both hands, slide your thumbs and fingers under the flaps on each side. Push up and bring the four outside points together in the center. The cootie-catcher will look like a star you can open and close with your fingers.

9. To add fortunes: Color code each of the four outside panels. Then open and flatten the cootie-catcher (so that it looks like the picture in step 6) and put a number on each triangle. Then lift each flap and write a different fortune in each of the spaces underneath.

10. To tell fortunes: Have the person pick one of the colors on the outside panels. Open and close the cootie-catcher one time for each letter in the name of the color. (For example, open and close the cootie-catcher three times for the color RED.) Then have the person choose one of the numbers showing inside the cootie-catcher. Open and close the cootie-catcher that number of times. Finally, have the person pick another of the numbers showing. Open that flap and predict the future!